This is a
happy book
all about
MARTHA –

that's me!

Come and see my
BRILLIANT new suitcase!
It's shiny and red and
it has wheels so I can
pull it along...

In it I'm packing

my scrapbook

Martha

and my pencil case

for my pencils

and my glue

and my scissors...

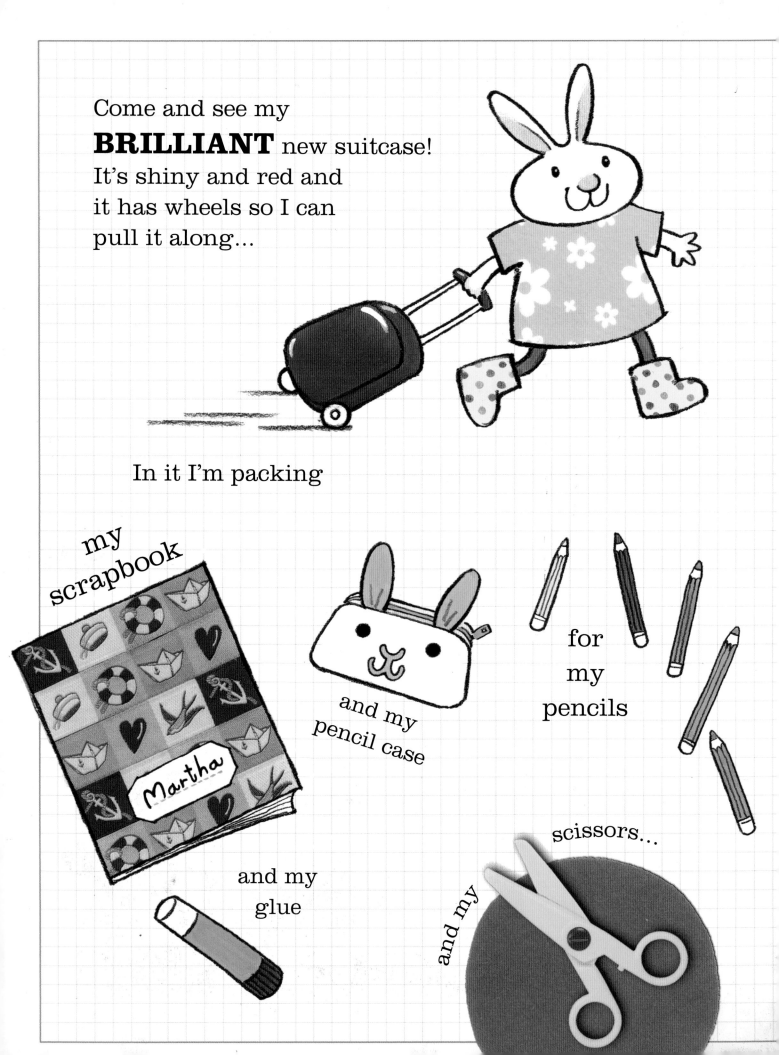

my bucket

and spade

and my starry sunglasses

and my **best** swimming things,

because –

News!
We are going on
holiday
to the seaside!

I am ready to go
right now!

But what about my **bunny brothers,**

Monty and Pip?

And our puppy Paws...

Will they **ever** do their packing in time?

"Come on **Monty!**" I say.

"**HURRY UP** Pip!

Mum and Dad are calling us!"

We

bring

all

our

things

and *rush* outside...

To where **Bluebell,** our camper van is waiting for us!

Inside it
is like a
little house...

It has curtains and a table and a tiny fridge
and lots of secret cupboards to put our things in...

and at bedtime the seats change by

magic

into BEDS!

When we are all in,
it's a bit
of a

squash.

At last –

beep beep!

we're off!

After A... G... E... S...  we say,

And Mum says,
"NEARLY there..."

We say,

"are we nearly there yet?"

And Mum says,
"YES!"

But **OH NO!**

t- r -a- f- f -i- c j -a- m

"are we nearly there yet?"

And Mum says, "NEARLY there..."

Then we say,

"are we nearly there yet?"

We play our best game, which is YELLOW CAR. We look out of the window and if we see a yellow car we shout, "Yellow Car!"

"LELLOW CAR!" says Pip

and THEN...

We arrive at the seaside!

I'm so **excited.**

Pip is wearing Mum's hat!

We all get ready to go into the sea... **BUT**...

When we dip in our toes –

it's **SO COLD!**

I say, *"let's swim!"*

but Pip says,

"DON'T WANT TO."

So I say,

"Okay. Let's look
for shells and
pretty pebbles…

and make a
**BIG
BUNNY
FACE…**

in the sand.

And then we will swim in the sea!"

But Mum says, **"it's lunchtime!"**

Luckily, I **LOVE** picnics.

I choose

a cheese sandwich   strawberry yoghurt   and apple juice

Monty chooses

a ham sandwich   peach yoghurt   and mango juice

and Pip chooses

an egg sandwich   banana yoghurt   and milk

There's SAND in my sandwich — but it still tastes SO GOOD!

After lunch,
our umbrella flies away…

Mum's hat
blows off…

and we bury Dad's legs –
until only his feet are sticking out!

Then I say, "*Let's go in the sea!*"

But Pip says,
**"DON'T WANT TO.
WANT ICE CREAM!"**
So I say, "Okay, ice creams.
And then we will go
in the sea."

I don't know
which one
to choose...

they
are **all** so yummy!

Pip drops his ice cream.

Dad gets him another one, but he drops that too.

Luckily,
I say,
"Have a lick of mine, Pip!"

Then – oh no – Paws
runs off with my
starry sunglasses,

and it takes **AGES**
to find where
he's buried them…

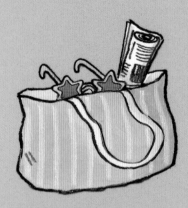

so I put them
in a safe place.

Then I say, "**NOW** let's go in the sea!"

But Pip says,
"**NO!**"

"Okay," I say.
"Let's have a competition to build the
BIGGEST and the **BEST** sandcastle!
And then we will go in the sea."

I have

a yellow
bucket

an orange
spade

and pretty
pebbles.

Monty has

a red
bucket

a green
spade

and some
seaweed.

and Pip has

a blue
bucket

a pink
spade

and a pine cone he
finds in his pocket.

"My sandcastle
is **BRILLIANT!**"
says Monty.

"FLAT!"
says Pip.

But my sandcastle is
extra special.
It has a moat and a bridge
and windows and stairs...

and best of all I fetch the bunny nose shell
from our **BIG BUNNY FACE**
and I put it on top.

"I WIN!"
I say.

"I WIN!"
says Monty.

"WIN!"
says Pip.

Then Pip jumps on
Monty's sandcastle...

Monty jumps on
Pip's sandcastle...

and Dad says,
"I don't like the look
of those storm clouds coming..."

Then my sandcastle gets jumped on too!

So I say,

"RIGHT!

I am going for my swim

ON MY OWN..."

Then I hear,
"Martha! Martha!
Wait for us!"

It's my
bunny brothers.

Pip says,
"I wet now! **SEA**!"

Luckily we don't care
about the rain!
We all hold hands…

and we go in the sea **together.**

While we are splashing and jumping in the waves...

the sun comes out!

When we are warm and dry,
me and Monty and Pip
and Mum and Dad and Paws
go back to Bluebell.

I unpack my shiny red suitcase,

and I do my
scrapbook.

At bedtime, we see the first
twinkly stars in the sky.

"Today has been GREAT!" I say,
"and tomorrow we will do it
all over again!"

"SEA!"
says Pip.

I love going in the sea...

But…
holidays with my
bunny brothers are what

I love best!

The End!